*If we took all of the children
for one hour per week and taught them
to focus on compassion then in one
generation all wars would stop.*

Dali Lama

Where do you want to go....

Imagine if you could
help a plant grow
just by sending it
your beautiful energy.

Wouldn't the world be so colourful?

Imagine if you could
sail the seas with a boat
you created with your mind
then when the sea got rough
your mind could turn the sails
into wings and you could fly away.

Where would you go?

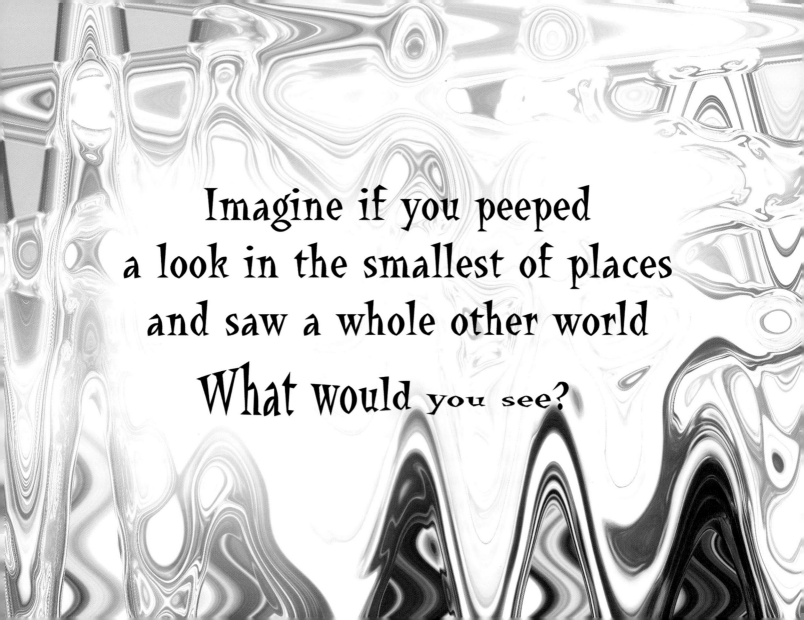

Imagine if you peeped
a look in the smallest of places
and saw a whole other world

What would you see?

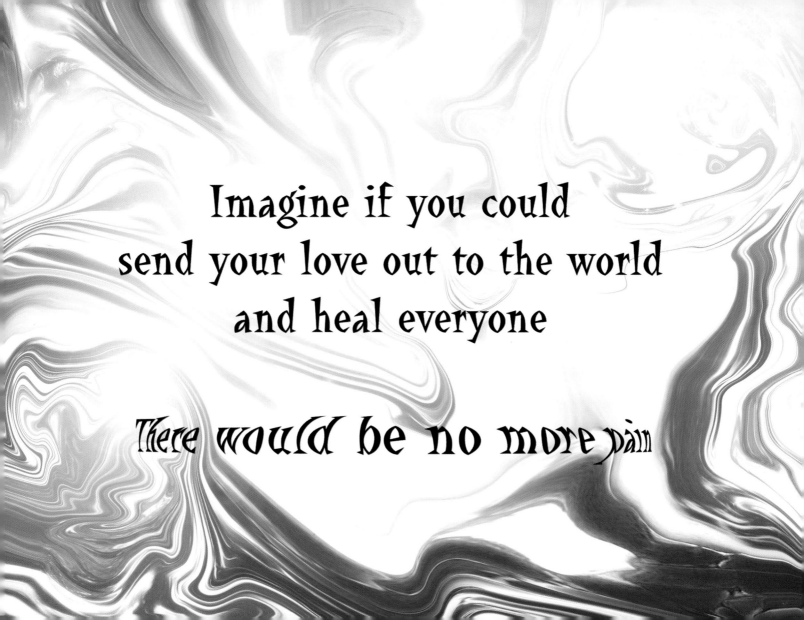

Imagine if you could
send your love out to the world
and heal everyone

There would be no more pain

Imagine if you could talk to the Earth
and she could talk back to you.

What
would
you
ask?

Mother Earth spoke through the rock formation of this picture, can you see the two hands holding?

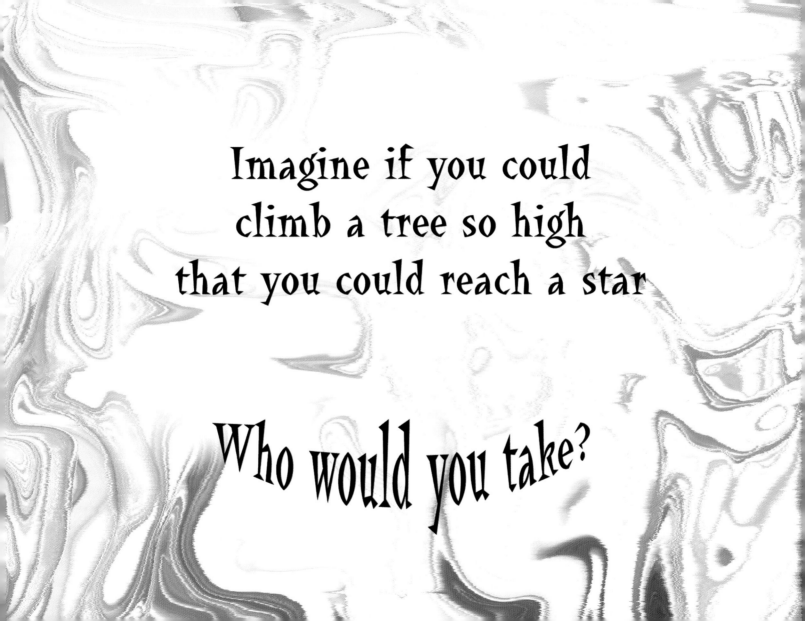

Imagine if you could
climb a tree so high
that you could reach a star

Who would you take?

Imagine if you could
talk to the animals

What would they say?

Imagine if you could
play with the universe

What would you create?

Imagine if you could create your own toys with energy around you and play with them

Your adventures would start with your mind

Imagine if you could ride the animals
of the sea's and they could
take you to all of their
secret places

I wonder where they would take you?

Imagine what the mushrooms really hide when your not looking?

Blink real quick and you might see a glimpse

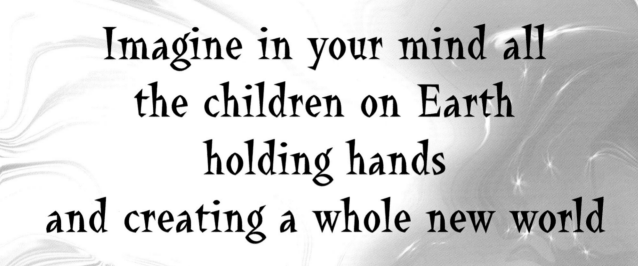

Imagine in your mind all
the children on Earth
holding hands
and creating a whole new world

A world where everyone is happy

Lets open your

Imagination

what do you see ?

What sort of life would you
like to live in?
Using your imagination create
whatever you would like by starting
up your very own imagination book,
find pictures, draw pictures, write,
what ever works for you,
there is no right or wrong,
only your amazing
Imagination

Author B.S.Richardson   Illustrator B.S. Richardson   Photographer B.S Richardson   Accompanying Photographer Nicole van der Burg